Danny's Bee
(the beginning)

written and photographed
by
Mia Coulton

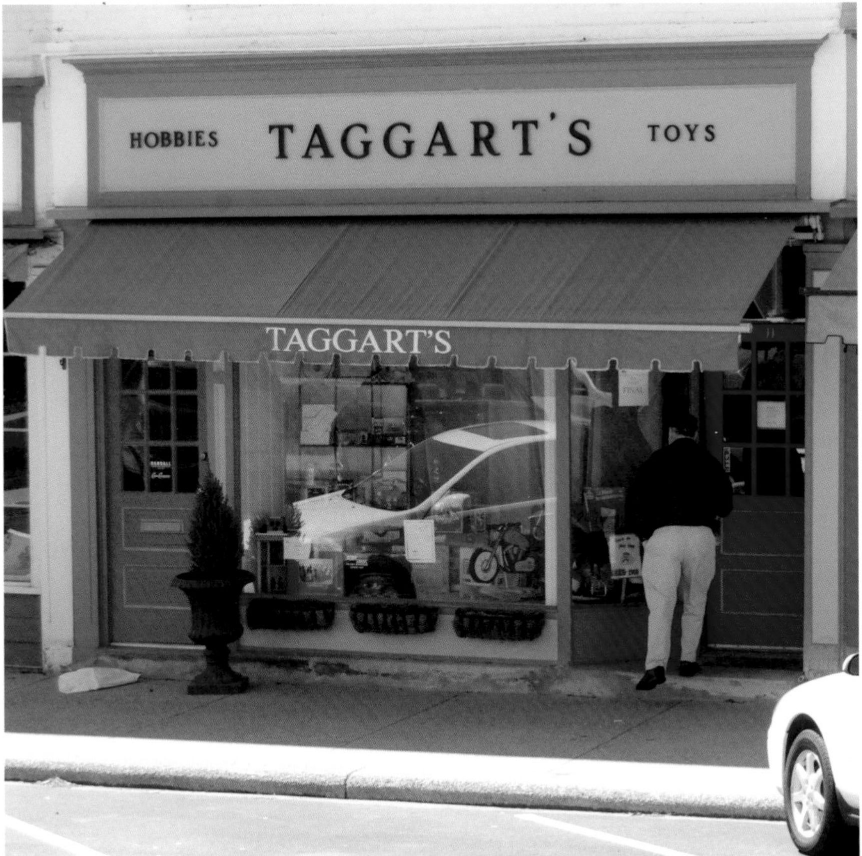
HOBBIES
TAGGART'S
TOYS
TAGGART'S

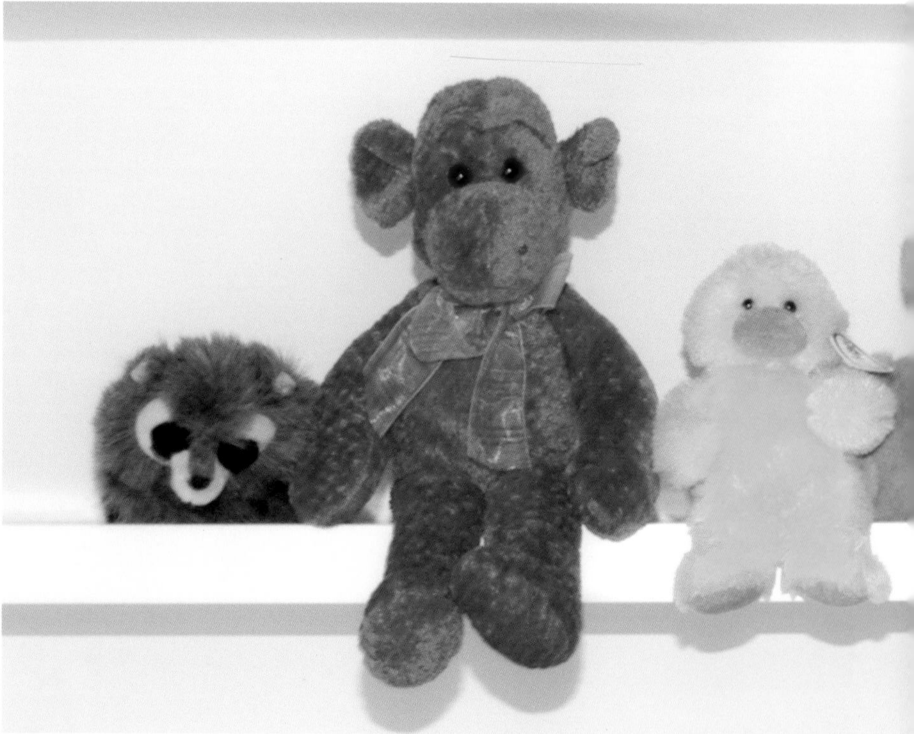

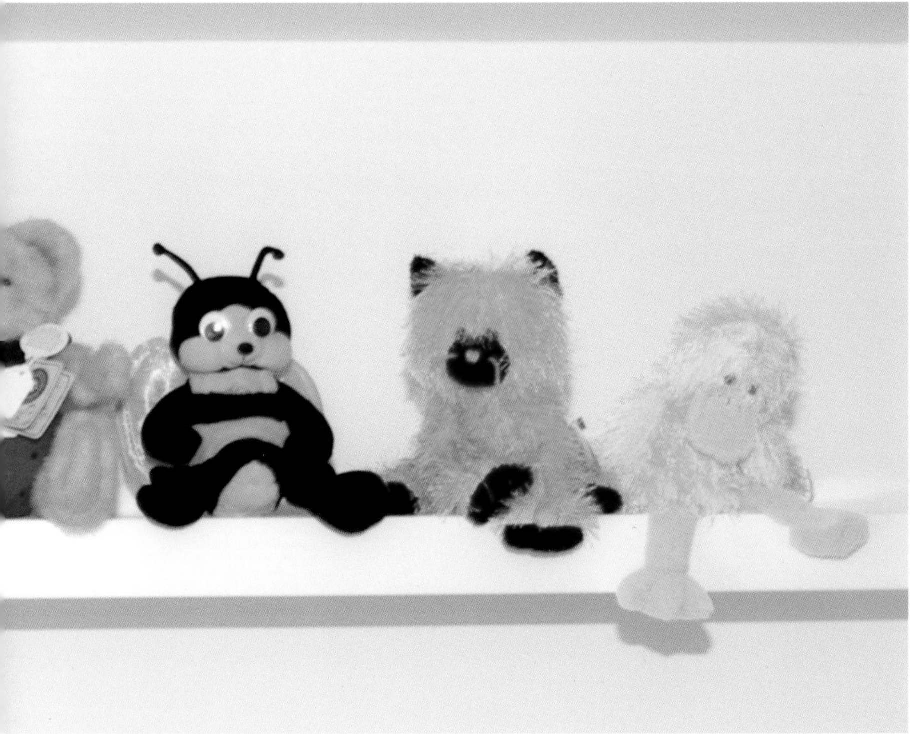

No.

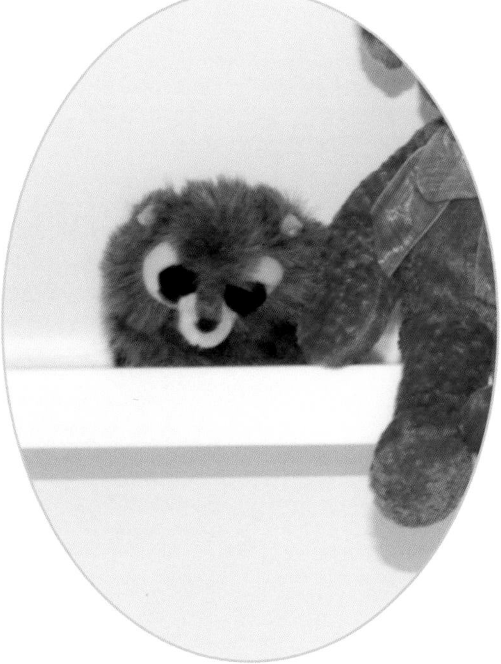

No.

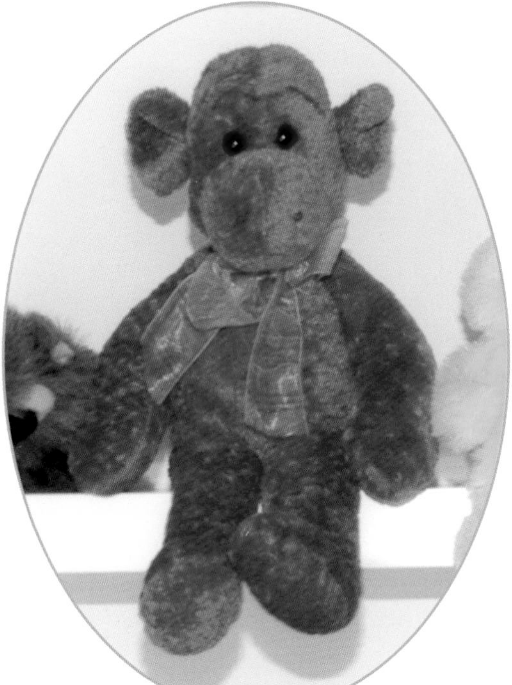

No.

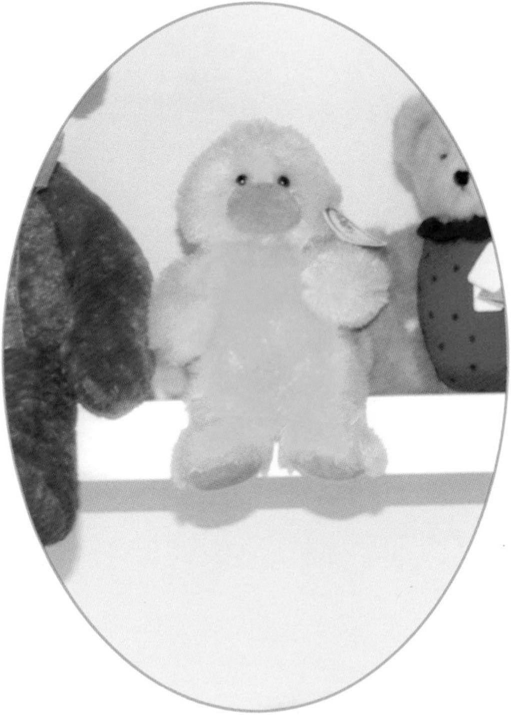

No.

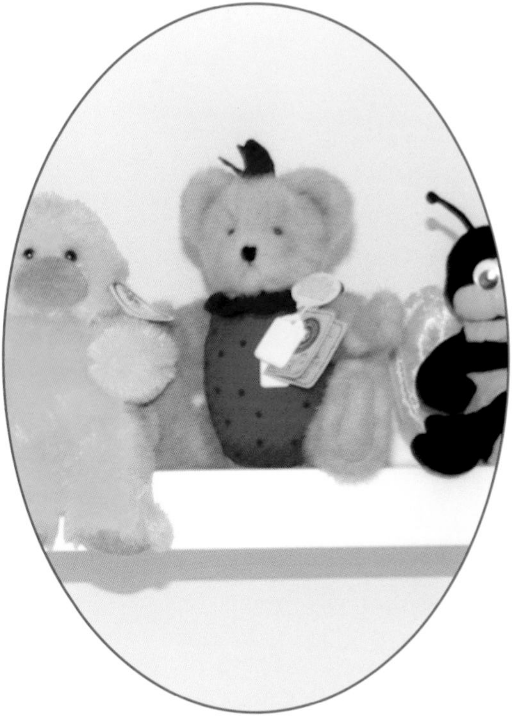

Yes!

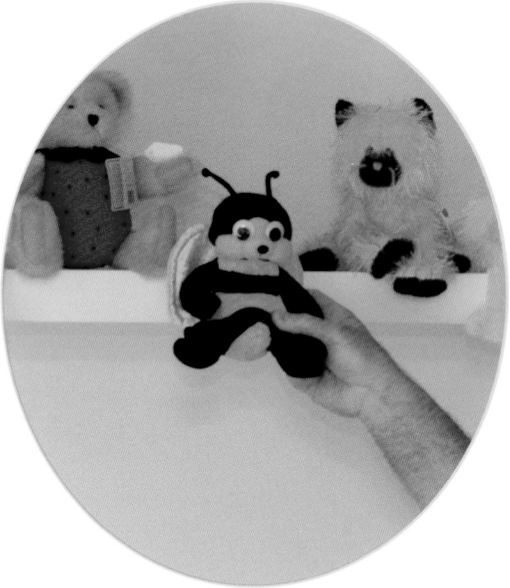

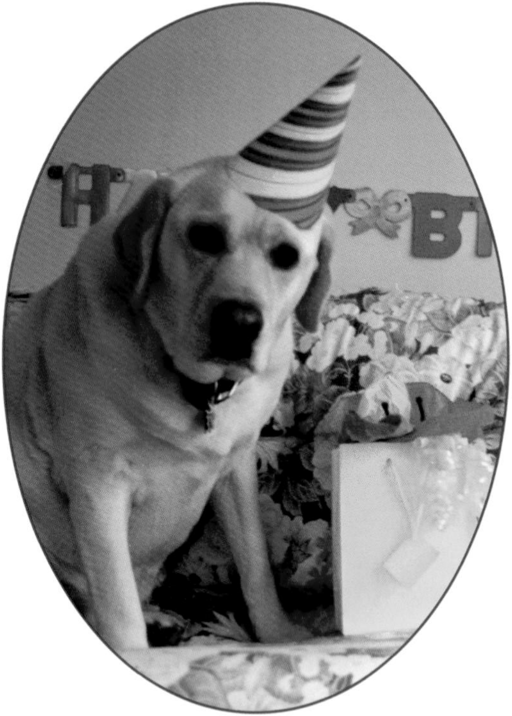